W9-CMS-784

HARALD AND THE GREAT STAG

FOR
BARBARA

Clarion Books
Ticknor & Fields, a Houghton Mifflin Company
Text and illustrations copyright © 1988 by Donald Carrick

Library of Congress Cataloging-in-Publication Data
Carrick, Donald.
Harald and the great stag.
Summary: When Harald, who lives in England during the Middle Ages, hears that
the Baron and his royal guests are planning to hunt the legendary Great Stag, he
devises a clever scheme to protect the animal.
[1. Deer—Fiction.   2. Hunting—Fiction.   3. Middle
Ages—Fiction.   4. England—Fiction]   I. Title.
PZ7.C2345Hb   1988   [E]   87-17875
ISBN 0-89919-514-8

H 10 9 8 7 6 5 4 3 2

HARALD AND THE GREAT STAG

DONALD CARRICK

Clarion Books

TICKNOR & FIELDS: A HOUGHTON MIFFLIN COMPANY

New York

The forest was forbidden to all but the Baron and his hunters. But the men who guarded it knew Harald. His father's farm was part of the Baron's lands, and he had been playing there since he was a child.

Often Harald brought the hunters a basket of berries, and they would entertain the boy with hunting stories. His favorite tales were of the Great Stag of the forest. He longed to see, just once, the brave beast that had earned the respect of all who tried to bring him to bay.

"I was certain the Stag was mine till he entered the stream," said one hunter. "The dogs were scattered for hours after they lost his scent."

"He saved his best trick for me," said another. "The big devil made tracks

for a field where the grass had been burnt. When the dogs' noses filled with ashes, the chase was over."

"Each year with the shedding of his antlers, The Great Stag seems to grow wiser and stronger," said the old hunter.

One morning Harald was walking toward a clearing where the largest berries grew. Birds and squirrels chattered in the trees while the early fog muffled his sounds below. Suddenly there was a loud rattling. Harald stopped. Through the mist he saw a deer step into the clearing, its antlers hitting the branches.

There stood the largest stag Harald had ever seen, its ears turning in search of threatening sounds. The majestic Great Stag was looking right at him. Harald tried not to breathe. He even tried not to blink, but he had to when his eyes began to water.

The next instant, the Stag snorted and disappeared back into the brush. It was like a dream.

Harald ran to find his friends, the hunters. He knew they would be proud of him when he told them what he'd seen. For despite the hunters'

stories, few of them had gotten closer to the Great Stag than his trail, or the scars on the beech trees where he sharpened his antlers.

The hunters were busy marking trails with twigs and gathering the pellets of stag droppings.

"I just saw the Great Stag," Harald blurted out.

"The lad brings a good omen," said a hunter. "This very day the Baron has declared a hunt."

Harald was confused. "Not for the Great Stag!" he said.

"You'll not see him again after today," said the hunter. "There's to be a purse full of gold for the one whose dogs bring him down."

"And a banquet afterward," added another.

Before, hunting had meant only stories to Harald. But now he had looked the Great Stag in the eye.

"It doesn't seem fair," said Harald. "All of you and your dogs to hunt just one stag."

The old hunter spoke. "It's always been that way, son." He pointed

toward the trees. "All of the animals in the forest are for the Baron's sport, and his alone. Their antlers are for his wall and their meat for his table."

He put his hand on Harald's shoulder. "The Stag is meant to lose, my boy. Better be off. It will go badly for you if you're caught during the hunt."

Sadly, Harald bade his friends farewell and left for home. When he reached the berry clearing, he paused. Harald could not forget the sight of the noble Stag. "I must help him," he thought. Harald knew that once the hunters had assembled at the Stag's trail, the dogs would be given the scent from the Stag's droppings and the hunt would begin.

Harald went to where the Stag had stood and gathered his droppings in the empty berry basket. Then he ran along deer trails, spreading the droppings on old tracks and new. He crossed and recrossed different trails, weaving a crazy pattern over the forest floor.

His basket was almost empty when he heard the dogs. The hunters were leading them to the Stag's trail. Harald couldn't run, or the dogs would see him. He crept into a hollow tree to hide until the yowling pack had passed.

Suddenly Harald realized he wouldn't be so lucky once the dogs had been given the Stag's scent. He was covered with it.

Harald ran to the brook. He hid his basket under the water and secured it with a rock. After washing hastily, he started for home.

There was a thunder of hooves. Horses were coming. The only direction Harald could go was deeper into the forest. Desperately, he scrambled up a large tree. Harald dared not move as the Baron and his men galloped past.

Horns sounded, announcing the start of the hunt. From his perch, Harald could see the small animals flee before the horns and dogs. Rabbits dashed this way and that. The din drove a night owl from its slumber.

A wary fox watched it swoop overhead through the trees. Harald caught the animals' fear. There would be no escape for them—or for him—till the hunt ended.

Several times the hunters coursed nearby. A hare froze as it had been taught; then, at the last moment, it bolted in panic. One of the dogs forgot itself to chase the hare, only to be chased, in turn, by the hunter, who returned it to the pack.

Harald dug his nails into the bark. He tried to shut out the hunt by closing his eyes, but the shrill horns and yelping would not let him forget it.

Below him, the hunters halted to regroup the pack.

"The dogs are confused," said one man.

"There's no clear trail for them to follow," said another.

Harald's heart beat faster when one of the excitable dogs circled his tree. It began leaping toward the branches. Harald clung even tighter, wishing he could sink under the bark.

The dog would not stop. Could it smell his fear? It began to attract other dogs. Harald wanted to strike out at the animal, but he was afraid of being discovered. It was horrible to be hunted.

Finally the old hunter stepped forward and pulled the dog away. "Stags don't climb trees," he said, and everyone laughed.

To Harald's relief the gathered dogs were let loose once more. But the sounds of the hunt still echoed up and down the forest, giving Harald no rest till dusk.

At last the forest returned to its normal small sounds. The evening animals began to feed. Harald dropped to the ground and walked swiftly toward home. He wondered if the Stag had escaped.

The old hunter was waiting at the forest's edge. "That was a brave thing you did, lad."

"You saw me in the tree, didn't you?" Harald said. The hunter nodded. "That's why you pulled the dog off."

The old man nodded again. "I thought you would want to know that your Stag still runs free," he said.

Harald's heart leapt. Then a huge smile spread across his face. "You've been his friend all along."

"Now he has two," the old hunter said as he slipped back into the forest.

One morning, a few months later, Harald noticed the Stag's print in the field near his house. Just down the row was a beautiful pair of silver antlers. The Great Stag must have shed them!

When Harald picked up the antlers they were still warm. His eyes searched the woods for the Stag, but he saw only shadows.